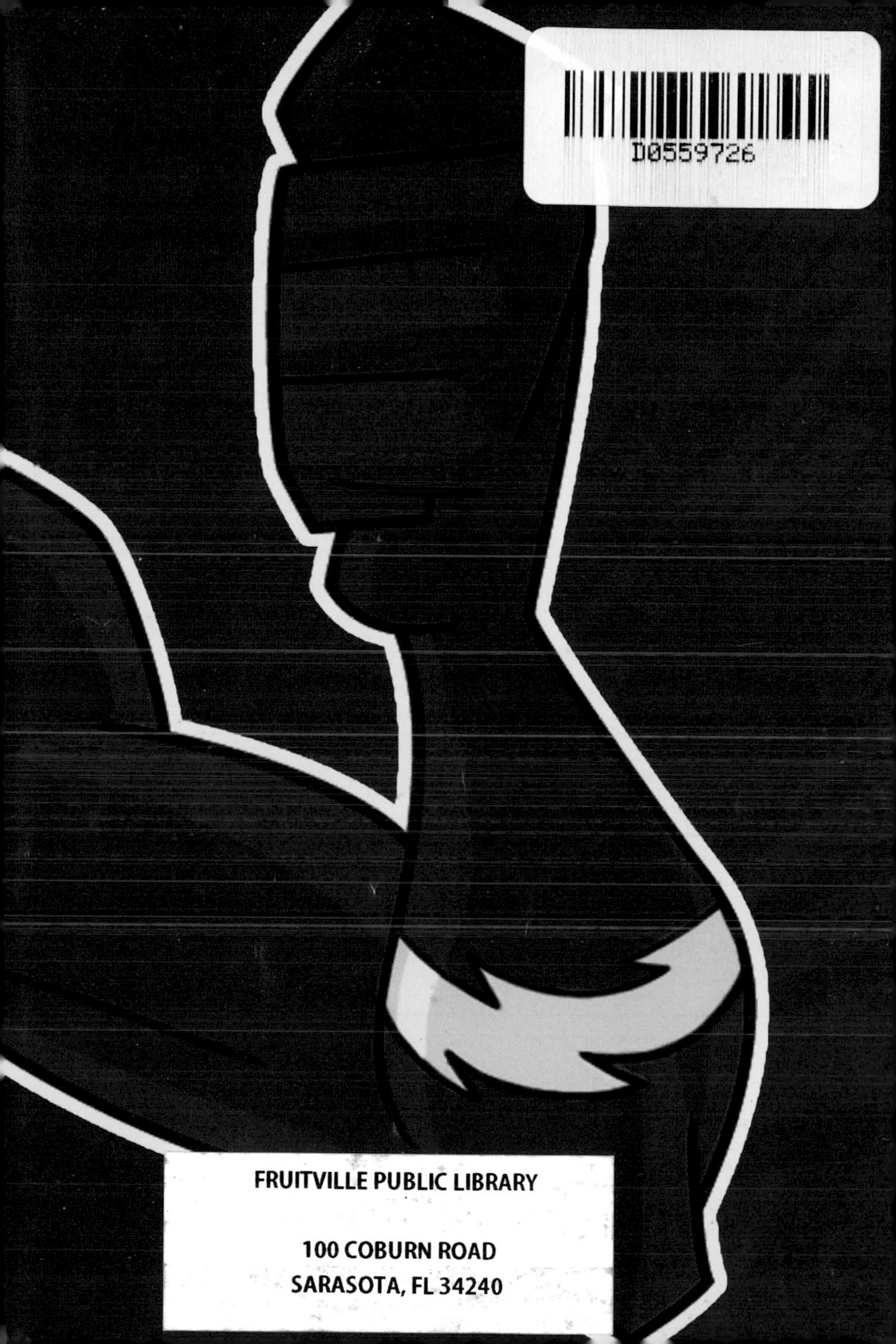

AFTER BEING STRUCK BY A BOLT OF LIGHTNING AND DOUSED WITH CHEMICALS, POLICE SCIENTIST BARRY ALLEN BECAME THE FASTEST MAN ON EARTH . . .

SUPER DC HEROES

The FLASH

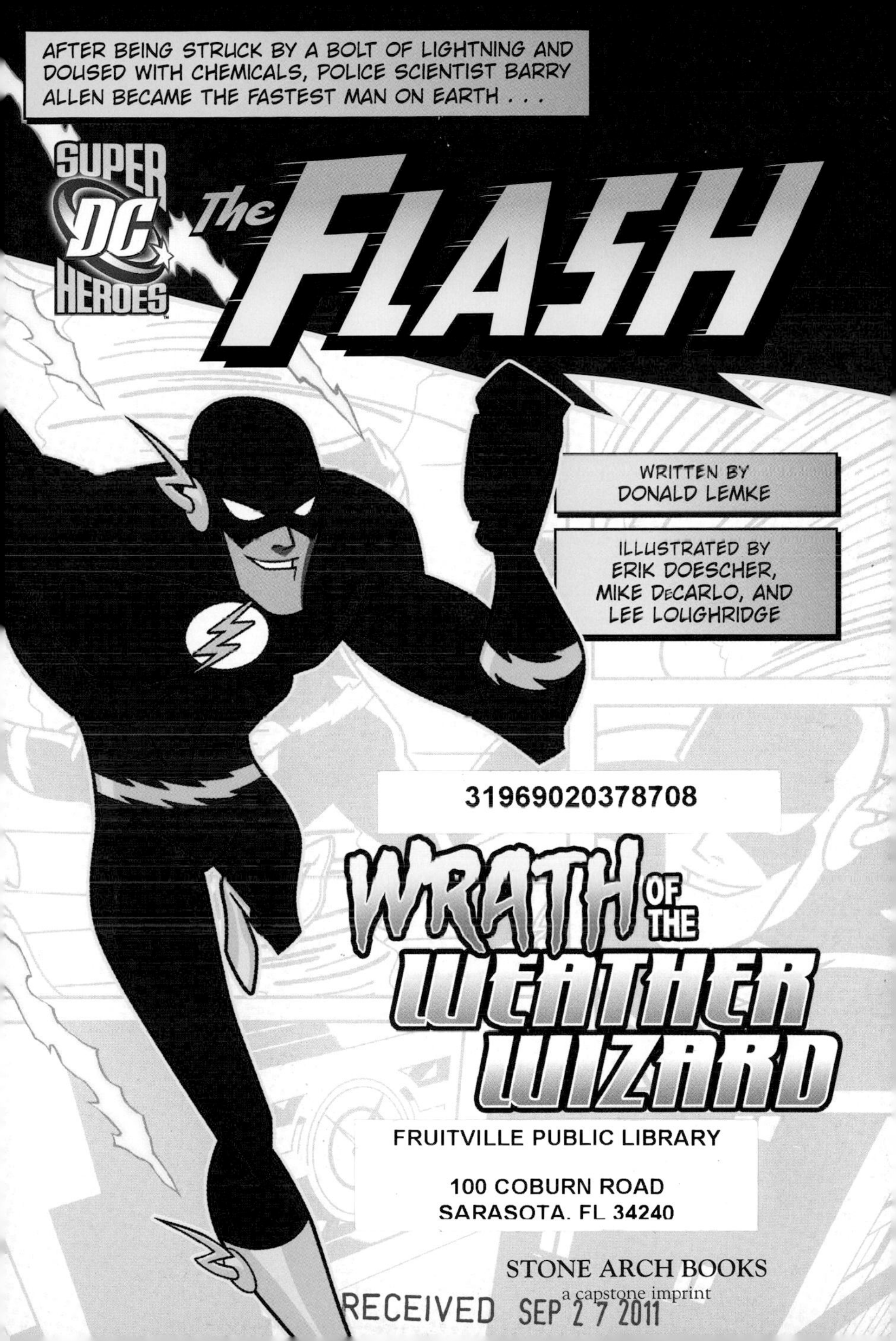

WRITTEN BY
DONALD LEMKE

ILLUSTRATED BY
ERIK DOESCHER,
MIKE DeCARLO, AND
LEE LOUGHRIDGE

WRATH OF THE WEATHER WIZARD

STONE ARCH BOOKS
a capstone imprint

Published by Stone Arch Books in 2011
A Capstone Imprint
151 Good Counsel Drive, P.O. Box 669
Mankato, Minnesota 56002
www.capstonepub.com

Library of Congress Cataloging-in-Publication Data

Lemke, Donald B.
 Wrath of the Weather Wizard / written by Donald Lemke ; illustrated by Erik
Doescher, Mike DeCarlo, and Lee Loughridge.
   p. cm. -- (DC super heroes. The Flash)
 ISBN 978-1-4342-2613-6 (library binding) -- ISBN 978-1-4342-3090-4 (pbk.)
 1. Graphic novels. [1. Graphic novels. 2. Superheroes--Fiction.] I. Doescher,
Erik, ill. II. De Carlo, Mike, ill. III. Loughridge, Lee, ill. IV. Title.
 PZ7.7.L46Wr 2011
 741.5'973--dc22   2010025594

Summary: On a hot summer day, the doors of Iron Heights Penitentiary
open, and the Weather Wizard walks out a free man. After years in prison, the
super-villain takes a deep breath and looks to the heavens. Suddenly, a giant
thundercloud erupts on the horizon! Across town, the Flash streaks toward
the storm and spots an F5 tornado threatening downtown Central City! The
Fastest Man Alive must save the city's residents and identify the cause of the
deadly twister. Until he does, the Weather Wizard will remain under a cloud of
suspicion.

Art Director: Bob Lentz
Designer: Brann Garvey
Production Specialist: Michelle Biedscheid

Printed in the United States of America in Stevens Point, Wisconsin.
092010
005934WZS11

TABLE OF CONTENTS

CHAPTER 1

CALM BEFORE THE STORM

After three years behind the cold steel gates of Iron Heights Penitentiary, Mark Mardon was a free man. The criminal's lawyer hadn't quite proven his innocence. However, she'd done enough to get his case overturned due to a lack of evidence.

Near the prison exit, a guard reached into a large envelope. He handed Mardon his belongings. By law, the police had to return all of his personal items, including a wallet, twenty dollars in cash, yellow sunglasses, and a titanium locket.

"What's this thing?" asked the security guard. He held up the mysterious piece of jewelry. "A lucky charm?"

Mardon took the locket and stared at it for a moment. Years ago, the criminal had hidden a tiny microchip inside the metal casing. The high-tech device would lead him to the weather-wand, an instrument able to control all of Earth's weather. With it, Mark Mardon became the super-villain known as the Weather Wizard.

"There's nothing lucky about it," Mardon replied. He placed the locket in his pocket and continued down the hallway.

The security guard followed. When they finally reached the exit, the guard swiped his ID card through an electronic lock. Then he looked back at Mardon, smiled, and pushed open the heavy double doors.

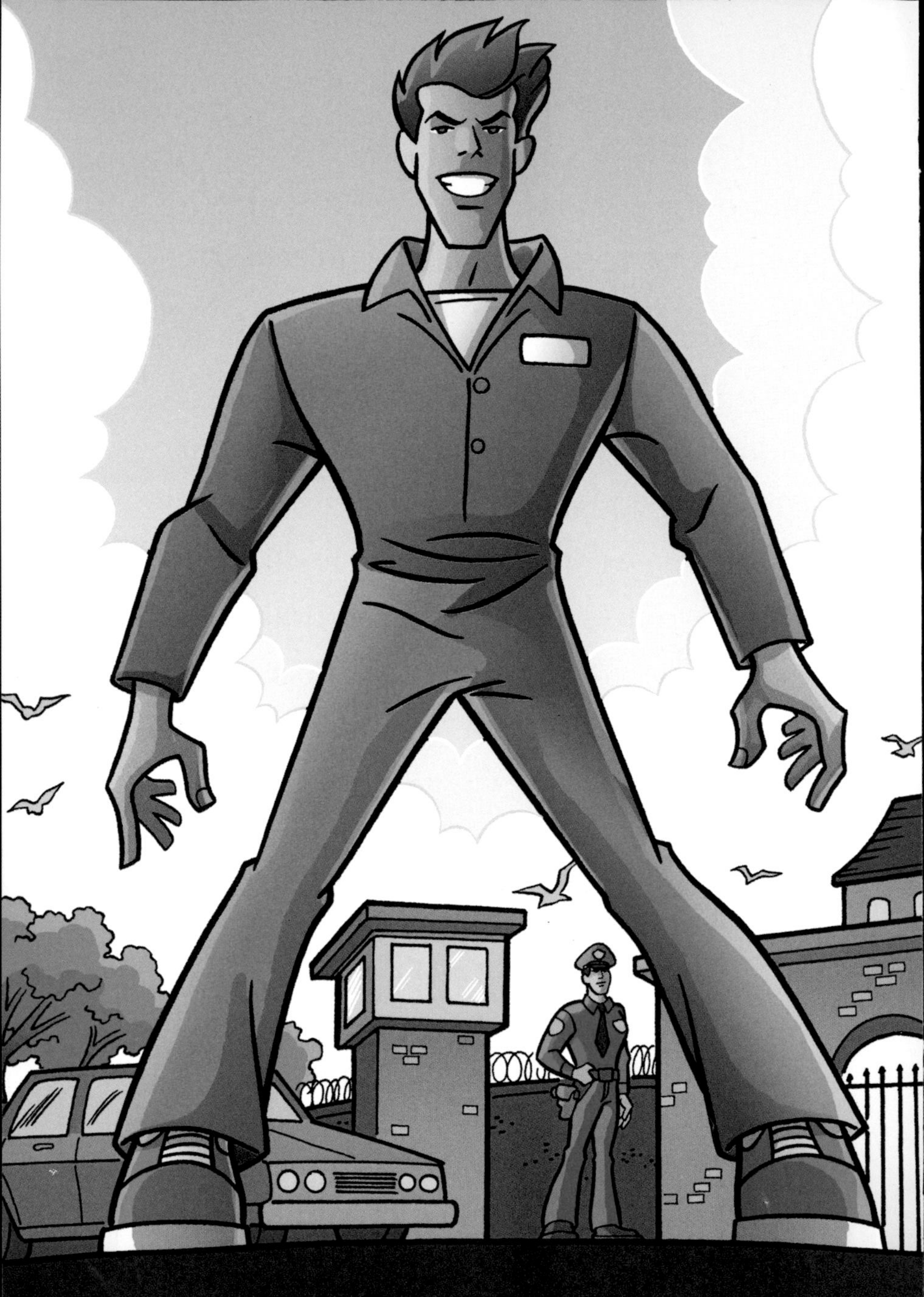

WHOOOOSH!

A blast of hot, humid air greeted the men. They stepped outside into the spring sunshine.

Mardon stopped, closed his eyes, and took in a deep breath of the warm air. The past three years had given him time to think. He thought about the crimes he had committed, his victims, and his family. But most of all, he thought about days like this one. He now knew his superpowers could do more good than evil. The weather could heal instead of hurt.

"You sure are calm," said the security guard. He watched Mardon enjoy his first breaths of fresh air. "You could've been stuck in there for forty more years. I'd be doing jumping jacks, if I were you!"

The words awakened Mardon. He opened his eyes and looked toward the heavens. Despite the bright blue sky, the Weather Wizard noticed a thick layer of black clouds creeping over the horizon. The villain's meteorological instincts told him that trouble was brewing.

"Calm," the Weather Wizard repeated. He placed his yellow sunglasses over his narrow eyes. Then he pulled out the titanium locket, gripped it tightly, and walked toward the darkening skies. *It's always calm before a storm,* he thought.

* * *

On the other side of Central City at police headquarters, Barry Allen placed a fingerprint scan into a high-tech computer and waited calmly. The database sorted through thousands of criminal files.

BEEP! BEEP! BEEP!

Within a moment, an alarm sounded. The machine displayed an image of the possible suspect.

"Got 'em!" Barry exclaimed.

As a police scientist, he'd identified hundreds of criminals from fingerprint evidence. Still, this case was particularly satisfying. After dozens of unsolved robberies, the suspect had finally made a mistake, leaving a small thumbprint on a grocery store cash register.

"He won't get away this time," Barry said to himself. "It's a perfect match."

Barry stared at the computer monitor. On screen, the images of two thumbprints glowed back at him — one from the cash register and one from the database.

The images were identical. Each had a pattern of thin black lines, which swirled out of the center like a tornado. Barry knew that twenty-five percent of the population had fingertips with these types of circular swirls, called whorls. He also knew that no two prints were exactly the same.

"Better get this information to the Chief," said Barry. He clicked Print on the computer. Then he walked toward the copier on the other side of the police lab.

BEEP! BEEP! BEEP!

"What now?" said Barry, annoyed by the alarm.

He spun back around, expecting to see some sort of print error displayed on his computer screen. Instead, he realized the alert had come from his desktop radio.

"This is a message from the National Weather Service," an electronic voice on the radio continued. "At about five o'clock, a powerful tornado touched down twenty minutes southwest of Central City, heading toward downtown. All residents are urged to take cover."

"Oh no!" shouted Barry. He rushed to the window of the police laboratory. In the far distance, he spotted a giant black wall cloud nearing the suburbs of Central City.

Barry had only moments to react. For him, however, a single moment was more than enough. Years earlier, during a similar storm, a bolt of lighting had made Barry the Fastest Man Alive. Now he would use those powers to save residents of his hometown.

Barry pushed a button on his high-tech ring. His super hero uniform sprang from inside. In a split second, he changed clothes and sped out of police headquarters.

WHOOOOSH! The Flash streaked toward the thunderhead.

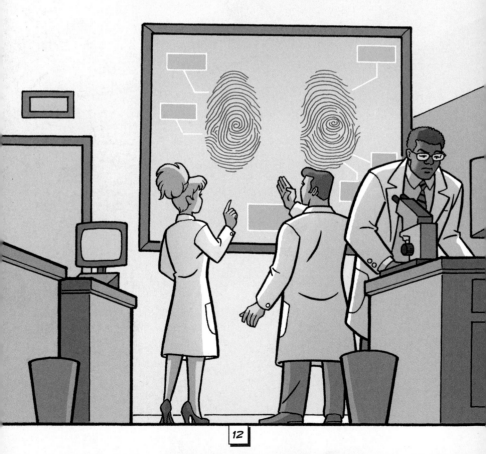

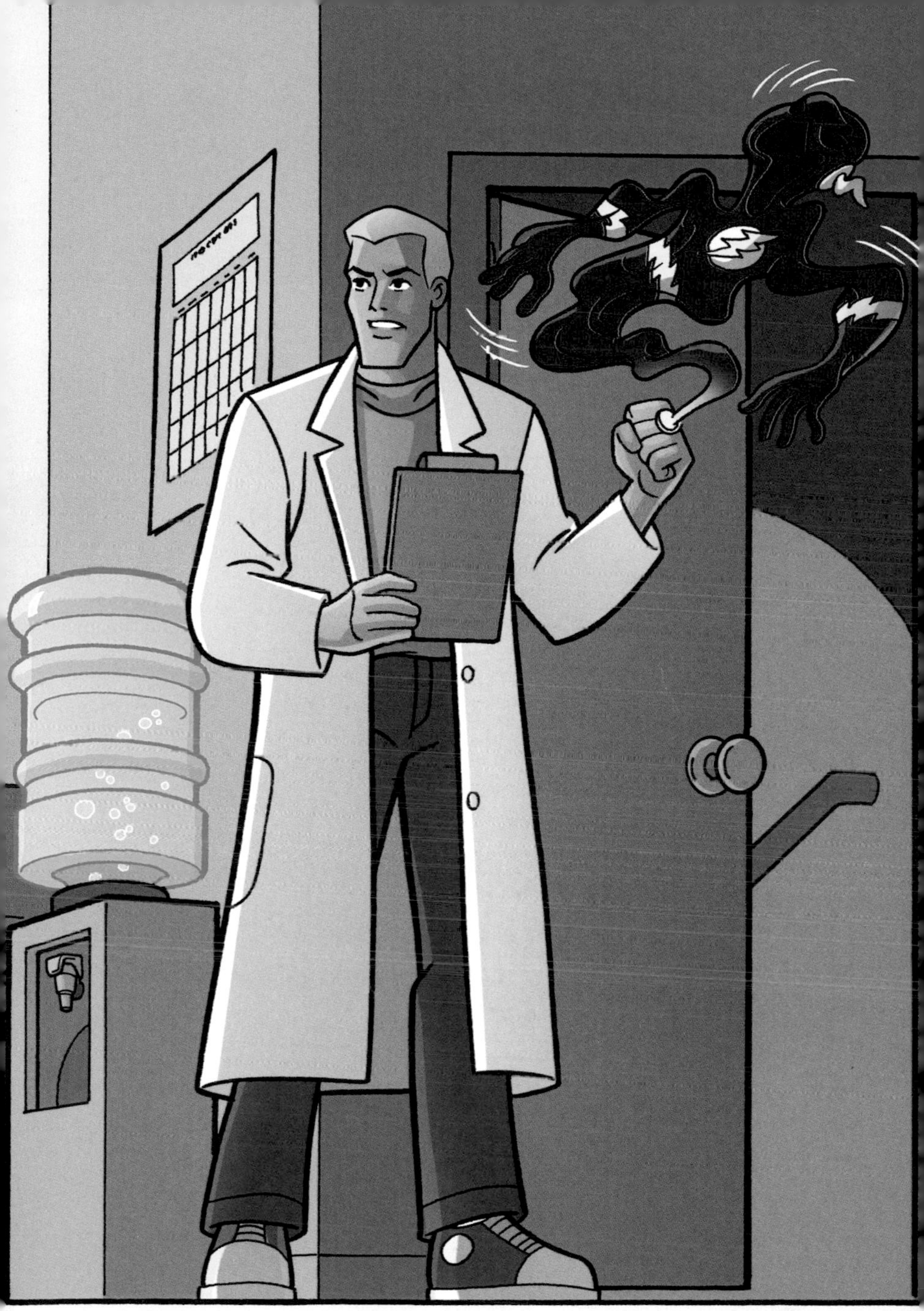

CHAPTER 2

A TWISTER OF FATE

Faster than a bolt of lighting, Flash zoomed into Central City. Heavy wind and rain whipped through the streets of downtown. People fled from their cars, seeking safety in the nearby buildings.

Between the skyscrapers, Flash caught a glimpse of the horizon. A greenish black funnel cloud continued its approach. From the size of the storm, Flash knew the city's buildings would offer little protection.

"I have to do something!" shouted the Scarlet Speedster.

ZWWWWOOOOMMMM! The super hero raced toward the twister. As he neared the deadly storm, hail pellets blasted him like bullets. The strong winds nearly slowed the speedster to a stop.

"Help us!" a woman shouted from nearby.

Through the wind and rain, the Flash could barely hear her repeated calls for help. **WHOOOOSH!** He rushed back and forth across the streets, trying to locate the shouts.

"Under here!" the woman said with one last effort.

Flash scanned the area again. Finally, he spotted the woman, lying beneath her car and cradling a baby. She was trying to protect her child from flying debris.

"Hang on!" yelled the super hero.

With the twister only a few feet from his back, Flash rushed toward the family. Then suddenly, a strong gust of wind lifted the woman's car into the air. **FWOOOSHHHHHH!** The vehicle spun into the sky like a helicopter blade. Just as quickly, it started falling back toward the street.

ZWWWOOOOMMMM! In less than an instant, the Fastest Man Alive scooped the woman and her child into his arms. **KRASSH!** The two-ton car slammed onto the street. But the super hero was already long gone. He sped toward downtown with the wind at his back.

When he stopped, Flash quickly set the family down in the safest spot he could find. Then he rushed back toward the twister before they could even thank him.

By now, the storm had become a powerful F5 tornado. Super-strong winds shattered windows, toppled trees, and tore the roofs off houses. The Flash knew he had to stop the deadly whirlwind — and fast.

The Scarlet Speedster raced at the tornado. **WHAM!** The violent storm spit the super hero onto the street like a chewed piece of gum. Flash tried once more. **WHAM!** Again, the twister spun him out like a top.

"Any more of that, and I'll be too dizzy to save the day," said Flash, holding his head.

Then suddenly, Flash had an idea. "That's it!" he exclaimed. "Tornadoes spin counterclockwise. If I spin in the opposite direction, I might be able to reverse the wind's rotation and stop this thing."

THWOOOOOMMMM!!

The Flash spun as fast as he could in a clockwise direction. When he was only a blur, the super hero leaped into the F5 tornado.

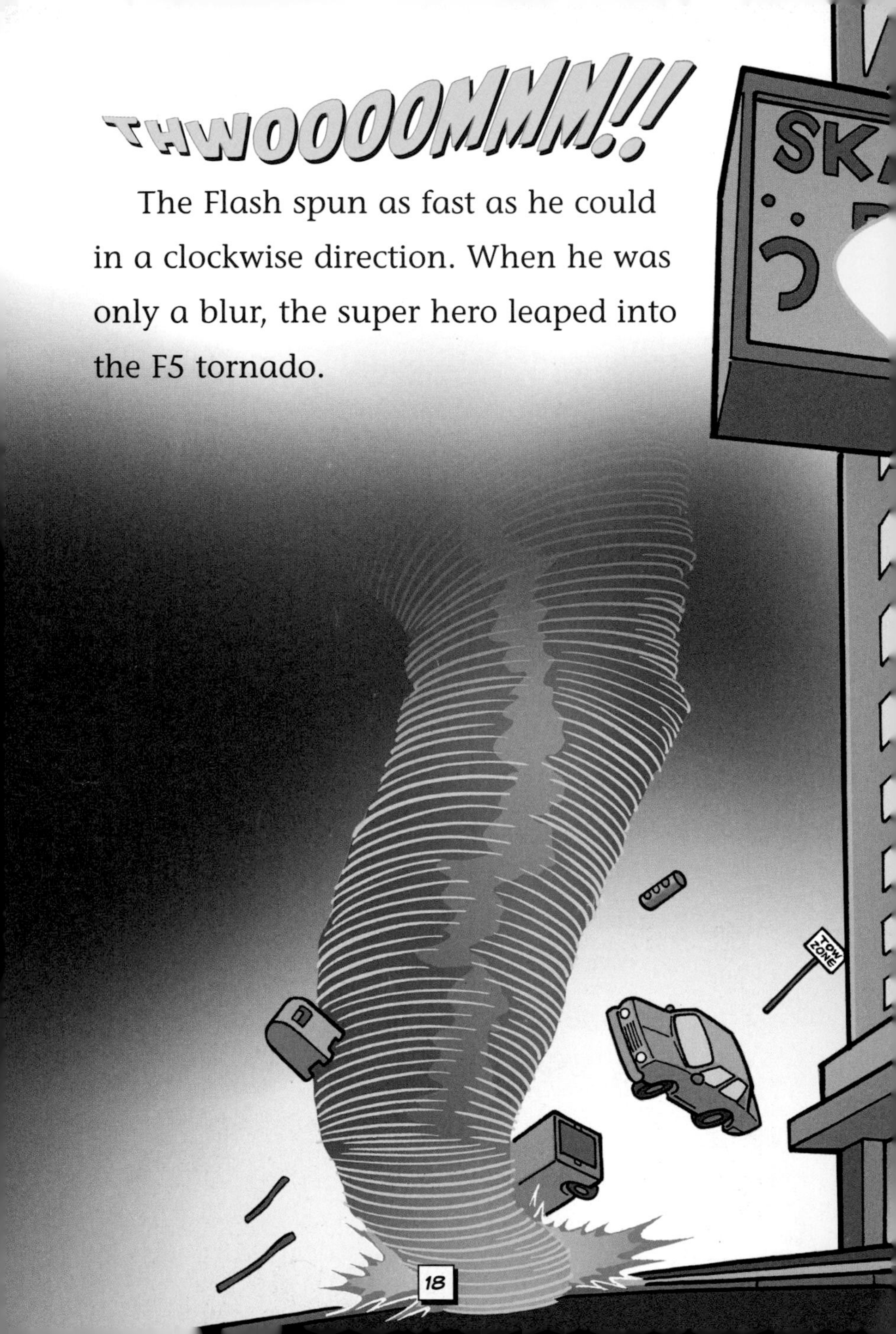
TOW ZONE

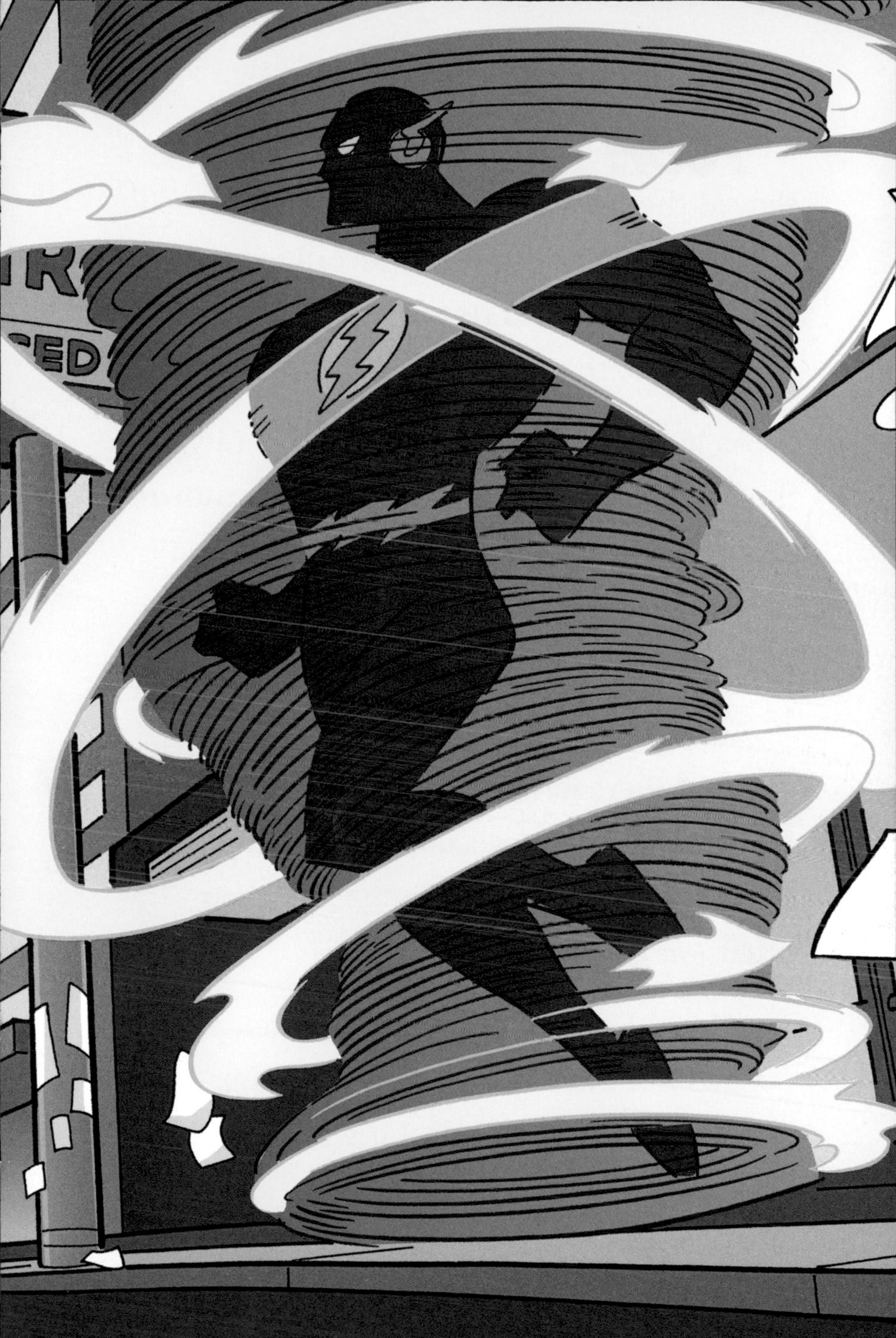

POOF! The force of the wind quickly slowed the Flash to a stop. **WHAM!** He fell to the street. This time, the deadly winds had been grounded as well. As fast as it had started, the tornado was gone.

As the skies cleared over Central City, the Scarlet Speedster returned to downtown. Residents emerged from their shelters, hugging each other and crying with joy. They were thankful to be alive.

As some began picking up the littered streets, others formed a crowd around the Flash. Television news crews that had been covering the storm quickly turned their attention toward their savior.

"Flash! Flash!" shouted a reporter. She pushed her microphone into the super hero's face. "Do you mind if we ask you a few questions?"

"Um," said the Flash, caught by surprise. "I guess that'd be fine."

"I got a question for ya!" shouted a voice from nearby.

Flash and the reporter spun around. A large man stormed toward them from behind. He waved a crumpled newspaper in his hand, which he had picked up off the street.

"What are you going to do about this?!" yelled the man. He shoved the newspaper into the super hero's face. The Flash quickly read the bold-faced headline. "WEATHER WIZARD TO BE RELEASED," it said.

The reporter read the headline as well. Then she turned back to the Flash with another question. "Is the Weather Wizard responsible for this disaster?" she asked.

"Of course he is!" shouted another man before the super hero could reply. "They never should have let that wacko out!"

"Slow down," said the Fastest Man Alive, words he rarely uttered. "Let's not jump to conclusions —"

But the crowd had already begun to chant. "Stop the Weather Wizard! Stop the Weather Wizard!" they shouted.

WHOOOOSH!

A moment later, the Flash was gone. The crowd cheered as he raced away into the distance.

Flash didn't know who to believe, but somehow he had to uncover the truth.

CHAPTER 3

A CLOUD OF SUSPICION

The Flash bolted out of Central City. He followed the path of destruction the tornado had taken. The storm had left behind a trail of shattered houses, twisted trees, and overturned cars.

This certainly looks like the work of the Weather Wizard, Flash thought. However, the Scarlet Speedster needed stronger evidence to send the super-villain back to Iron Heights.

Twenty miles outside of the city, the tornado trail stopped in a small field.

Flash quickly skidded to a stop as well. Lying at his feet were his first clues in the case.

"Would you look at that?" the Flash said to himself. The super hero kneeled on the ground. A fifty-foot swath of cornstalks had been flattened by the storm. The stalks fanned out in a circular pattern, swirling from the center point like a whorl.

"Just like a fingerprint!" the Scarlet Speedster exclaimed.

Although the winds had disappeared, Flash quickly remembered that all storms leave a distinct signature. The direction of downed trees, the damage left behind, even the length of a tornado's path were clues of a storm's origin.

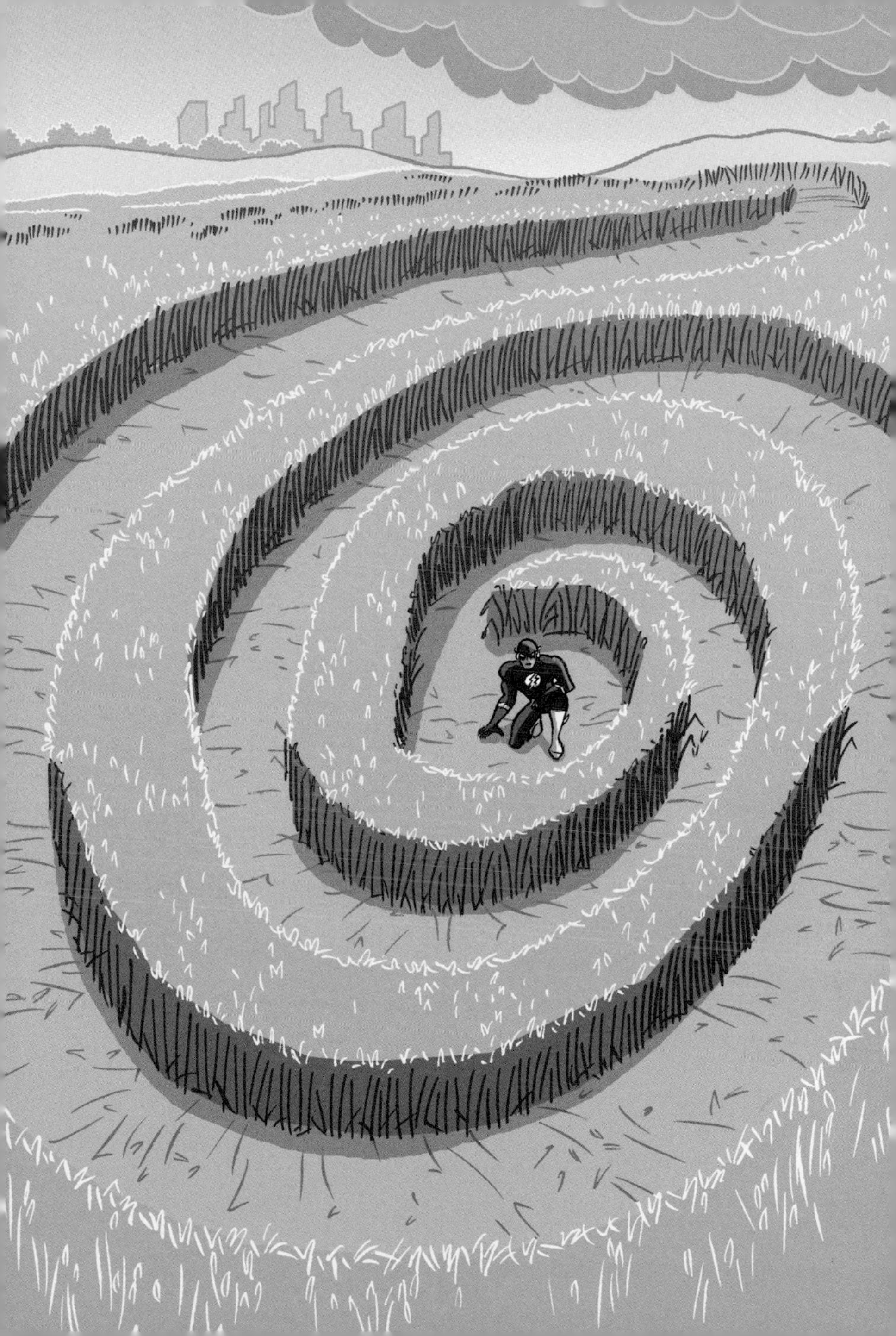

WHOOOOSH! Without a second thought, Flash raced back toward Central City. This time, however, he clocked himself and kept track of his speed.

When the super hero arrived downtown, the crowd was gone. The crumpled newspaper the angry man had shown him remained on the ground. The Flash picked it up and read the headline again: "WEATHER WIZARD TO BE RELEASED." Then he quickly scanned the remainder of the article.

"At 5:10 PM, convicted felon Mark Mardon will be released from Iron Heights Penitentiary," the report began. "After months of appeals, a judge overturned the case due to lack of evidence. Mardon will remain at the Central City halfway house until further notice. . . ."

"Exactly as I thought!" said the Flash. He threw the newspaper into a recycling bin and looked at his watch. A time of 5:24 p.m. glowed on the digital display.

Faster than a supercomputer, the Flash calculated the numbers in his mind. "The tornado traveled twenty miles at sixty miles per hour," said the super hero. "At that speed and distance, the storm would have started at exactly 5:04 p.m. — six minutes before Mark Mardon got out of prison!"

THUUUOOOMMMMM!! The Flash sped off. For the first time ever, the Weather Wizard needed his help.

Moments later, the Scarlet Speedster arrived at the Central City halfway house. The high-rise building was home to many former criminals, each trying to readjust to life outside prison.

The public, however, wasn't about to give the Weather Wizard a second chance. A large mob had already surrounded the building. They pounded on the doors and continued to chant.

"Stop the Weather Wizard! Stop the Weather Wizard!" the crowd shouted.

The Flash knew he couldn't convince the mob that Mardon was innocent. He needed to speak with the Weather Wizard himself.

The super hero zigzagged through the crowd at supersonic speed. To the average man, woman, and child, he was nothing more than a brief burst of wind. Reaching the front door, the Flash vibrated his molecules with unmatched quickness. As his molecules separated, he passed through the door like a phantom. VROOOOOM!

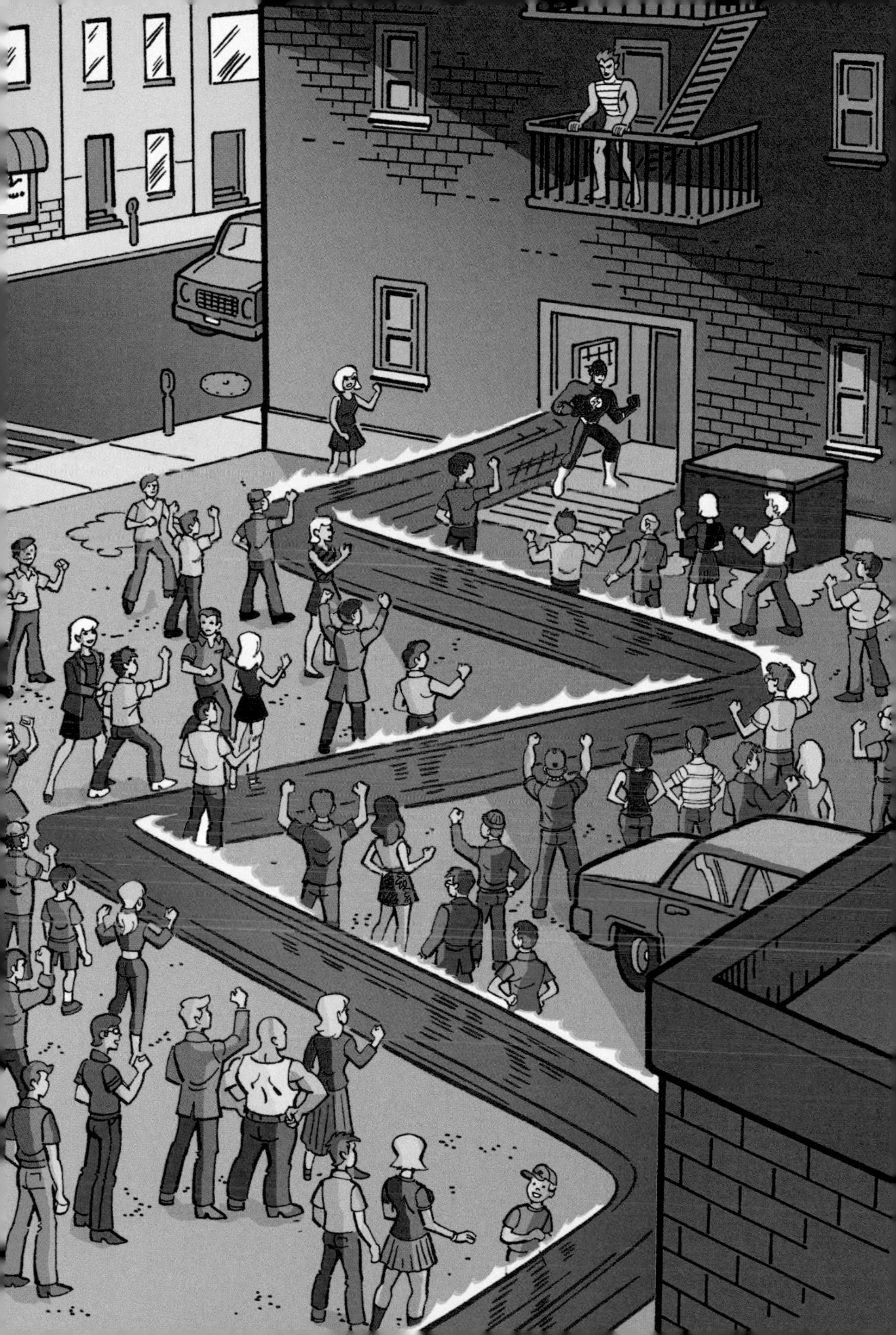

Once inside, the Flash rushed up several flights of stairs. He quickly passed in and out of apartments, searching for the Weather Wizard. Finally, he found him.

"I've been expecting you," the villain said. Standing at his apartment window, he removed the tiny microchip from inside the titanium locket. He screwed the device into his weather-wand, which had been hidden in a secret location.

"You didn't do it," said the Flash.

"Tell that to them," the Weather Wizard replied, looking down at the angry mob.

"I will," said the super hero. "Just give me time."

"Time?!" shouted the Weather Wizard. The villain spun around and faced Flash. He gripped the weather-wand in his hand.

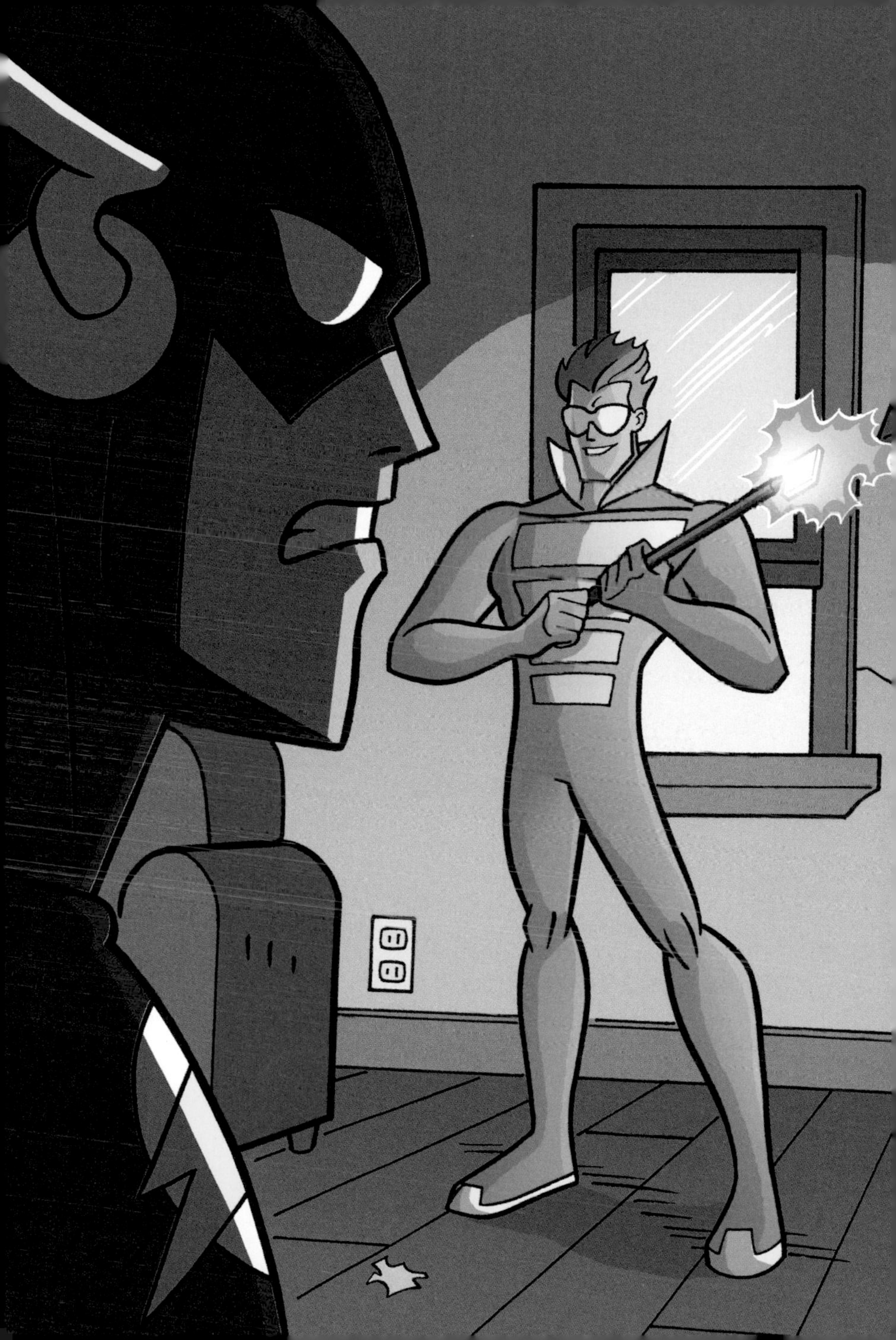

"I've done my time!" said the Weather Wizard. "I'm never going back!" The villain leaped out of the window.

"No!" the Flash exclaimed.

The super hero rushed to the window. He looked down but saw no sign of the Weather Wizard. **CLANK! CLANK! CLANK!** Then he heard footsteps coming from above. The Scarlet Speedster turned his gaze upward and saw the villain climbing the metal fire escape.

ZWWWOOOOMMMM! The Flash chased him onto the rooftop.

"What are you doing?" shouted the super hero. He watched the Weather Wizard grab onto the apartment's lightning rod. This tall, metal spire protected the building from lightning strikes.

Flash knew protecting Central City was the last thing on the super-villain's mind.

"It will never stop!" replied the Weather Wizard. "Even if I wanted to change, the weather won't let me."

"But I have evidence —" Flash began.

"And what about the hurricanes this summer, or the snowstorms this winter?" asked the villain, raising his weather-wand into the air. "Will you have evidence for those as well?"

"If that's what it takes," Flash replied.

A single raindrop fell from the sky. It landed on the Weather Wizard and trickled down his face like a tear.

"I don't think so," said the villain. He pointed his weather-wand at the lightning rod and fired.

KA-BOOM!

The spire erupted with electric energy and shot into the sky. A white light jumped from cloud to cloud, crackling in every direction.

The Weather Wizard stared up at the sky. Then he looked back at Flash and smiled. "I will, always and forever, be a force of nature!" declared the super-villain.

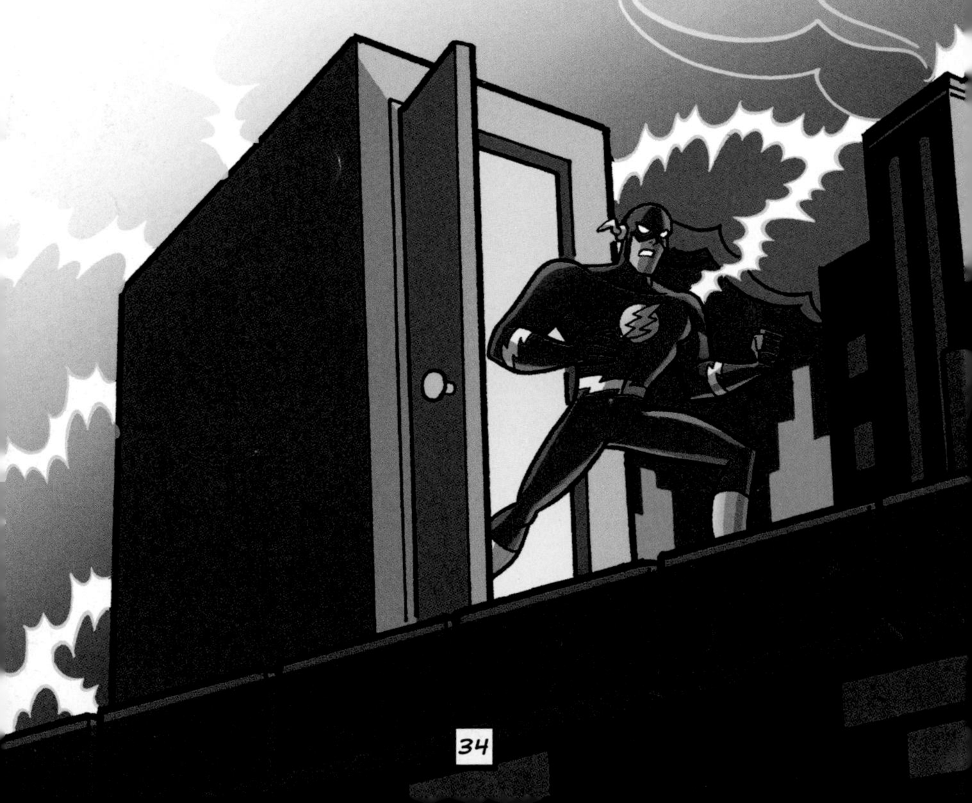

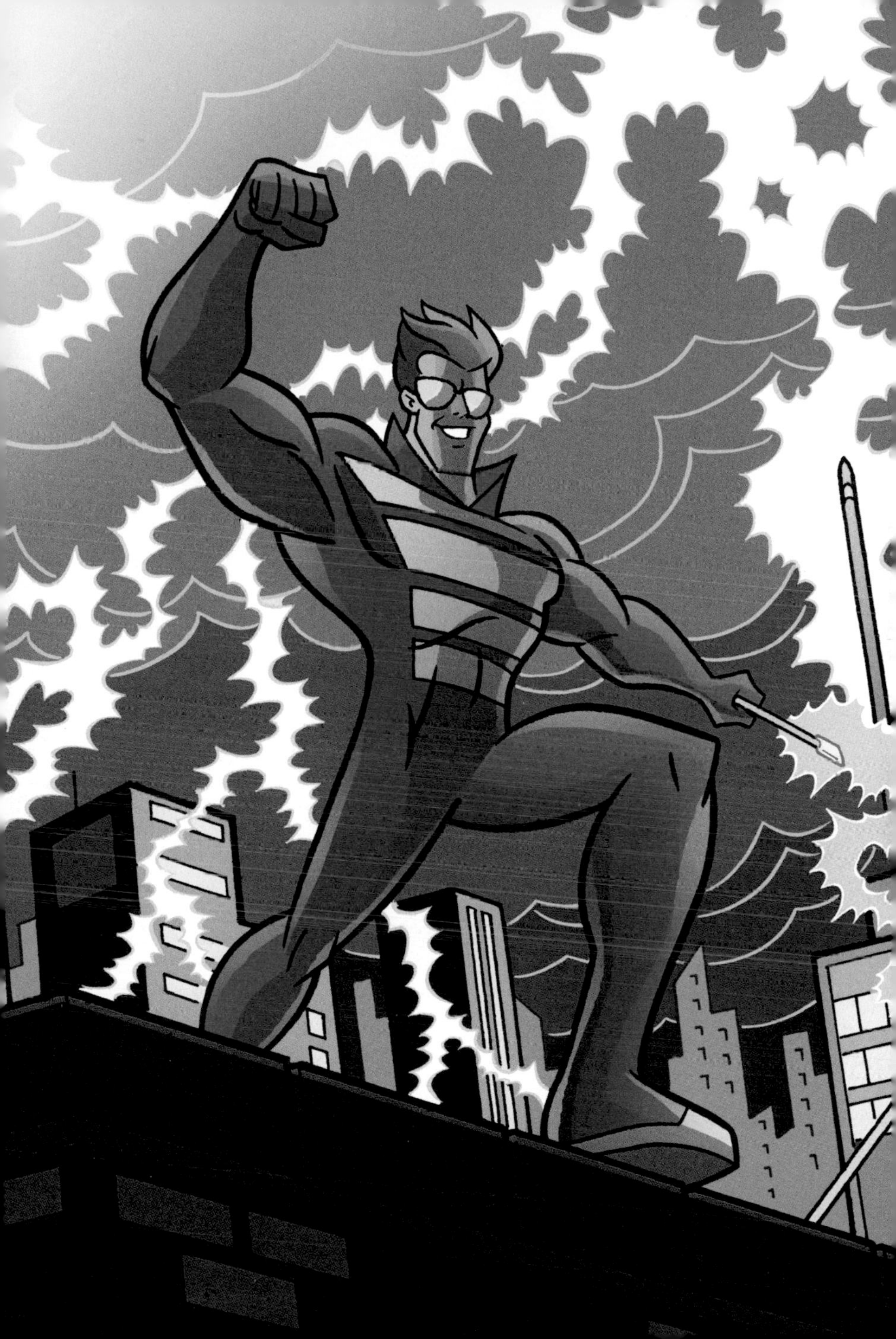

CHAPTER 4

SEVERE WIZARD WARNING

CRAAAAACK! As the Weather Wizard continued firing his wand into the lightning rod, bolts of electric energy poured from the sky. The bolts exploded on the city streets like grenades. Asphalt and cement flew in all directions. Car windows shattered. Mailboxes soared into the air. People scattered, fleeing for cover from the deadly weather.

On the rooftop, the Flash moved toward the Weather Wizard. "Stop this!" he shouted at the villain. "I can help you."

"Ha!" the Weather Wizard laughed. "I'm not the one who needs your help now."

SPLASH! A waterfall of rain spilled from the sky.

Flash peered over the edge of the roof. Within moments, the streets flooded into raging canals. Rushing water carried cars, trucks, and people toward a nearby river.

"Oh no!" exclaimed the Flash. Without hesitating, the super hero ran down the side of the apartment building.

He splashed into the flooded streets. Then the Scarlet Speedster quickly surfaced. In a blur, he ran across the surface of the water, moving too fast to sink.

WHOOOOSH!

Along the way, Flash scooped up dozens of people in a matter of seconds.

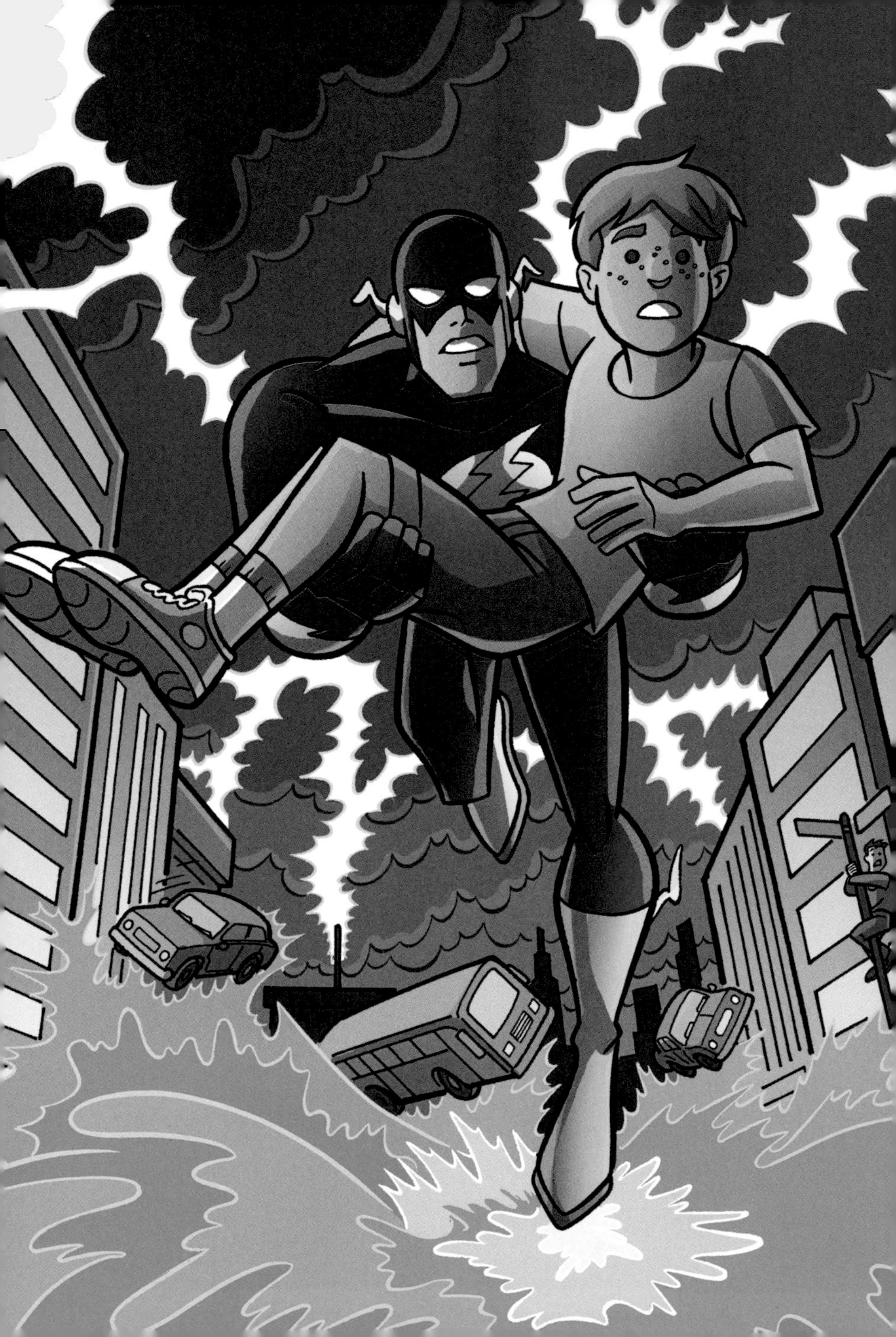

"Thank you," people cried as the super hero placed them out of harm's way.

The Flash didn't have time to celebrate. Before he could return to the rooftop, he heard the super-villain call out from above.

"You might be fast enough to run on water," shouted the Weather Wizard, "but let's see how you deal with ice!"

KA-POW! The villain shot another bolt of energy into the lighting rod, and the sky exploded again. This time, cold arctic air blasted through the streets of Central City. Rain turned to snow. The floodwater crackled, popped, and froze solid.

Suddenly, Flash was skidding along the icy streets, unable to stop himself. "Uh-oh!" said the Flash, heading toward a nearby skyscraper.

The super hero crashed into the building's thick glass walls. When he tried to get up, the Fastest Man Alive slipped and fell again on the ice.

After a third attempt to stand, the Flash tried a different approach. He placed his hands together and rubbed them back and forth at super-speed. *WHOOOOSH!* Incredible friction quickly heated the super hero's hands to nuclear temperatures. Then, placing his hands in front of him, he cut down through the ice like a wedge.

When his feet hit solid ground, Flash started to spin. *WHIR-WHIR-WHIR-WHIR!* The super hero spun so fast his entire body glowed like a swirling pool of molten lava.

The ice quickly turned to water and then to steam. Soon a thick layer of fog covered the streets like a blanket.

From high above on the rooftop, the Weather Wizard looked down upon the city. Every building and person had vanished beneath the fog. His main target, the Flash, was nowhere to be seen.

"Where are you?!" screamed the Weather Wizard.

"I'm right here!" said the Flash, suddenly arriving on the scene.

"Huh?" exclaimed the villain. He spun around with surprise, lost his grip on the lightning rod, and fell to the rooftop.

"It's over," said Flash. The clouds above the hero began to part. A bright ray of sun cast his shadow onto the cowering villain.

"Give up now," Flash said, "and it will be easier for you."

"Thanks for the tip," replied the Weather Wizard. "But I've got a slightly different forecast."

The villain raised his wand and fired directly at the Flash. **BANG!** The super hero quickly dodged the bolt of energy. **BANG! BANG! BANG!** The Weather Wizard missed again and again, as the Scarlet Speedster raced in circles around the rooftop.

The Flash knew he couldn't stop. If he did, the Weather Wizard would quickly strike him down. Instead, the super hero sped up, circling faster and faster around the villain.

ZWWWOOOMMMM!

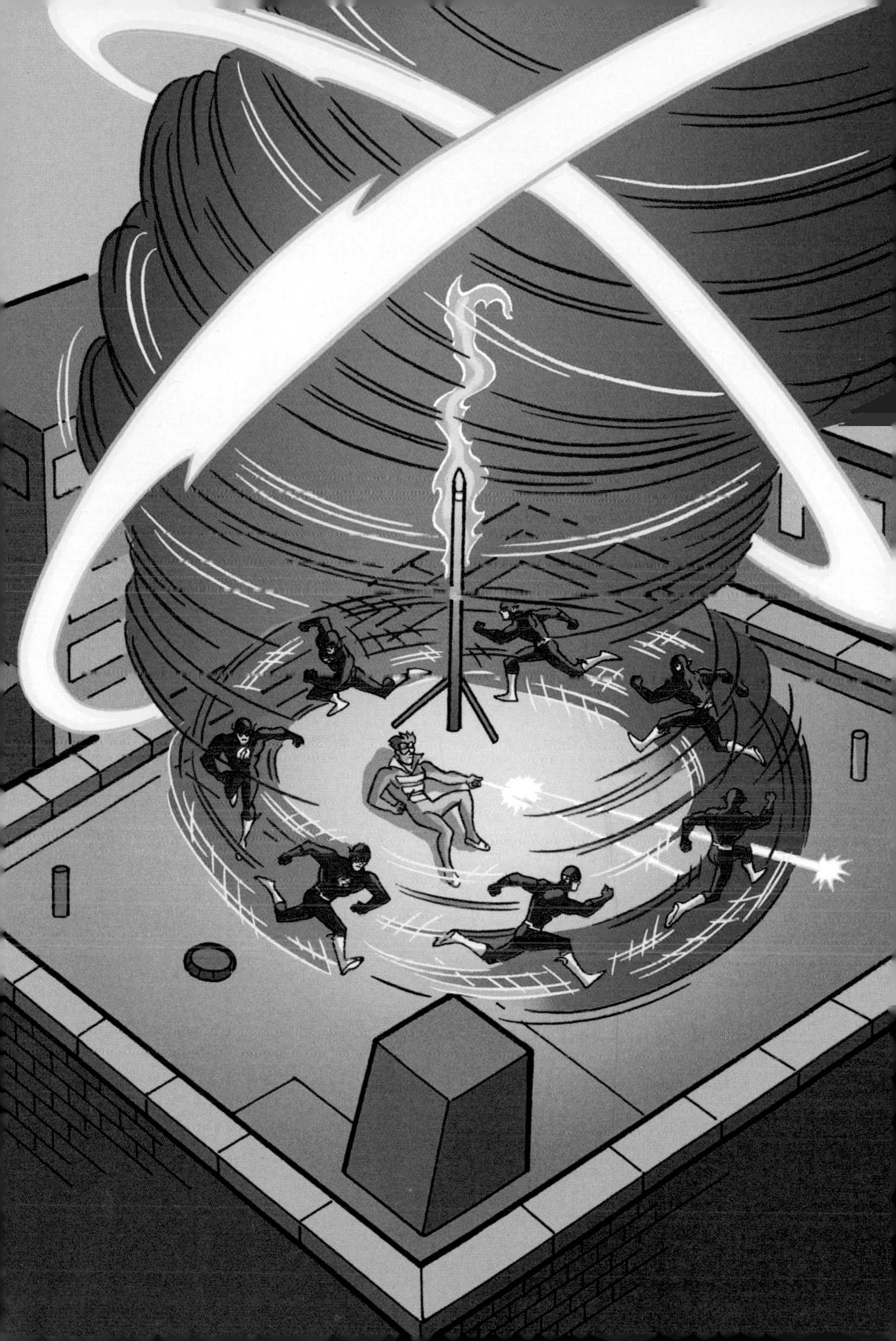

As his speed increased, the air around the Flash began to swirl. Soon, a reverse funnel of wind had formed on the rooftop. It pulled air from the ground and sucked it up into the sky. Within moments, the thick layer of fog blanketing the city twisted up through the whirlwind and spread harmlessly into the atmosphere.

On the streets of Central City, a crowd cheered for their super hero. But the Flash couldn't stop to accept their applause. He raced faster and faster around the Weather Wizard. The reverse tornado of air grew and grew.

"Stop!" the villain cried out from the eye of the storm. "I can't —"

Violent gusts of wind swirled around the Weather Wizard, but inside the tornado was like a vacuum.

All the air on the rooftop had been sucked into the sky. The villain had nothing left to breathe.

"I . . . can't . . . breathe!" The Weather Wizard spit out these final words. Then he choked for one last breath and fainted onto the rooftop.

The Flash immediately came to a stop. The funnel cloud quickly disappeared, and the air returned. The super hero rushed to the Weather Wizard's side. The villain had started to breathe again.

Before the Weather Wizard could awaken, the Flash grabbed his weather-wand. "*Now* it's over," said the super hero.

The sun bathed Central City in a warm, yellow light.

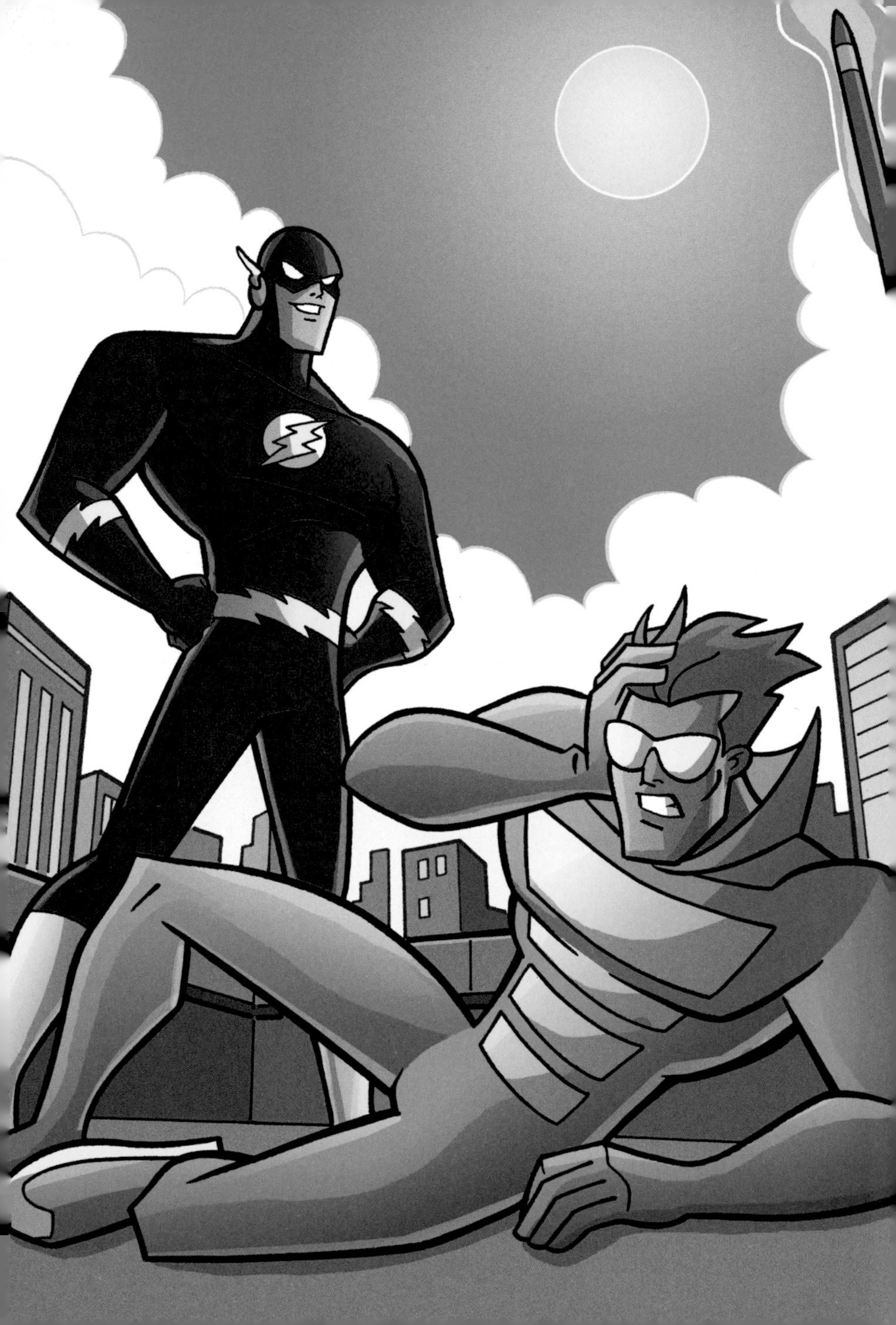

CHAPTER 5

STORM CELL

A few hours later, the Weather Wizard awoke. Dazed and confused, the villain shielded his eyes against a bright, white light from above. He looked around at the surroundings, and soon realized he was once again inside Iron Heights Penitentiary.

"He's up," said a prison guard standing outside the cell. The guard motioned for a visitor to come forward. "You got ten minutes."

The Flash stepped out of the shadows and leaned against the prison cell bars.

"How you feeling, Mark?" questioned the super hero.

"I'm not in the mood to chat, if that's what you're asking," the Weather Wizard replied.

"I got you a view," continued the Flash. He gestured toward a small, one-by-one foot window on the back wall of the cell. "It points east."

"So what?" said the villain.

"There are new days ahead, Mark," replied the Flash.

"Don't kid me," said the Weather Wizard. "I'm in here for life."

The Scarlet Speedster couldn't deny the super-villain's response. "This all could have been avoided," he said.

"In their eyes, I'm guilty," said the Weather Wizard. He turned and looked out the tiny window at the distant Central City skyline. "Eventually, every one of them would have turned against me again. Haven't you learned anything? You can't stop a growing storm."

The Flash shook his head. "I just did, Mark," said the super hero.

As the Flash turned and left, Mark Mardon grasped the cold, metal bars of the prison cell window. Looking up at the clear, blue sky, the hair on the villain's knuckles stood on end. He felt a new power growing from within, fueling a new anger. Then suddenly, a few wispy black clouds appeared overhead.

"My name is the Weather Wizard," he said.

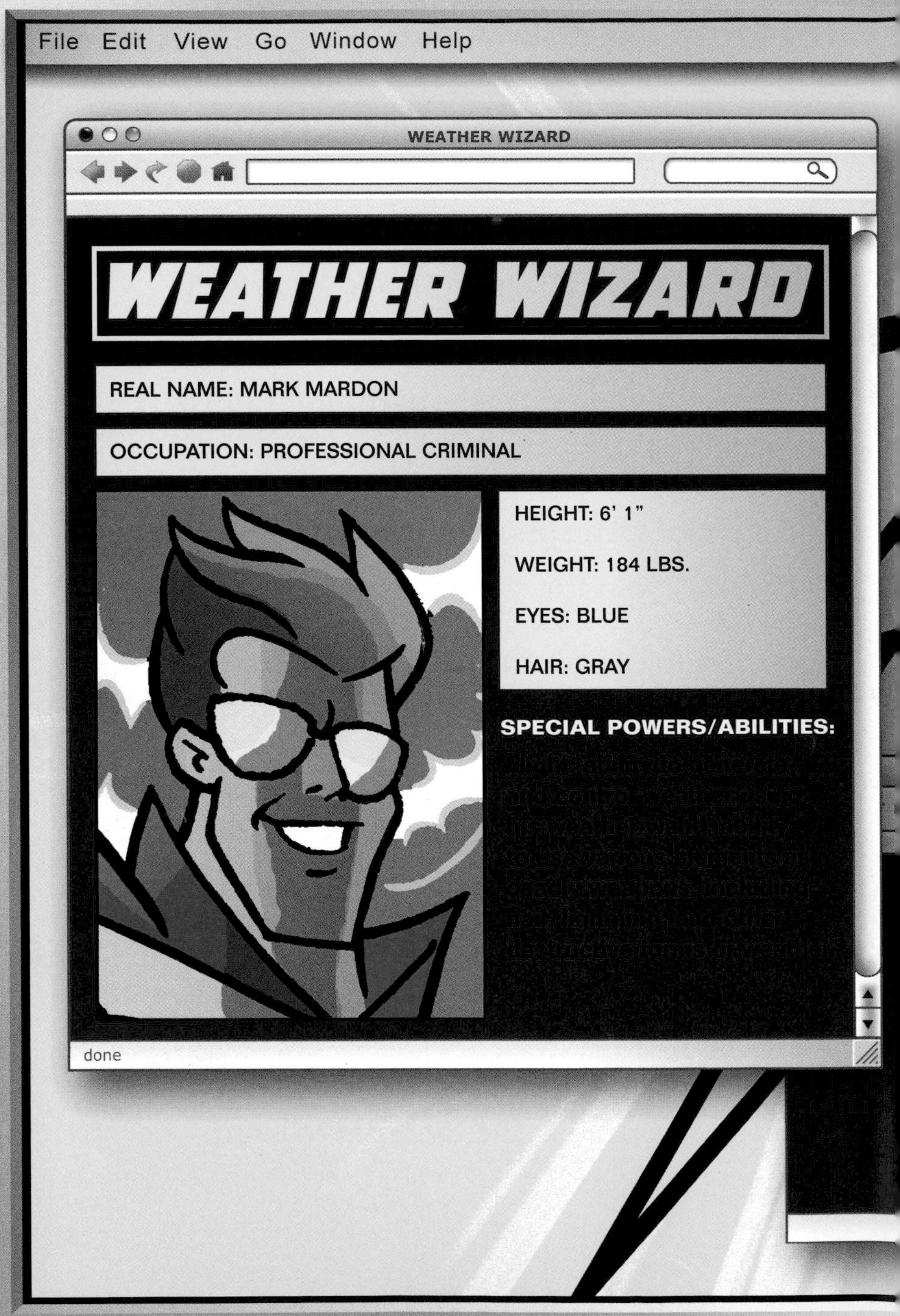
File Edit View Go Window Help
WEATHER WIZARD
WEATHER WIZARD
REAL NAME: MARK MARDON
OCCUPATION: PROFESSIONAL CRIMINAL
HEIGHT: 6' 1"
WEIGHT: 184 LBS.
EYES: BLUE
HAIR: GRAY
SPECIAL POWERS/ABILITIES:
done

Tue 6:23:12 PM Barry Allen

WEATHER WIZARD BIO

BIOGRAPHY:

One night, while running from the law, Mark Mardon hid out at his brother's house. His brother, a brilliant scientist, had just developed a device to control Earth's weather. He planned to use this weather-wand for good but never got the chance. That night, the siblings fought and Mardon's brother died. No one knows if the death was accidental. But Mardon fled, stealing the weather-wand and using the device to continue his life of crime. Nowadays, he considers Captain Cold and the Rogues his only family.

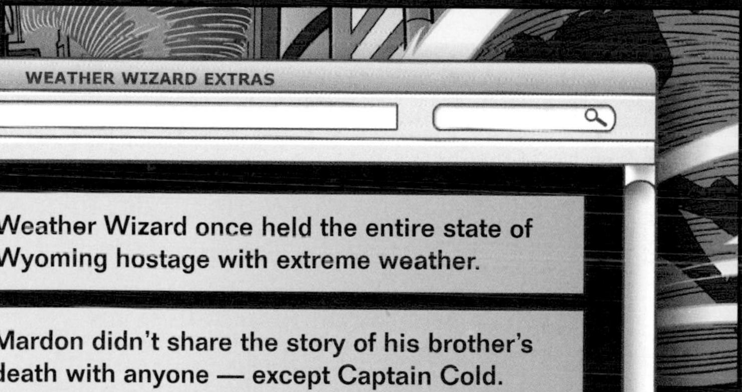

WEATHER WIZARD EXTRAS

Weather Wizard once held the entire state of Wyoming hostage with extreme weather.

Mardon didn't share the story of his brother's death with anyone — except Captain Cold.

Mardon's brother built the weather-wand for a super hero, but nobody knows who.

BIOGRAPHIES

Donald Lemke works as a children's book editor. He is the author of the Zinc Alloy graphic novel adventure series. He also wrote *Captured Off Guard*, a World War II story, and a graphic novelization of *Gulliver's Travels*, both of which were selected by the Junior Library Guild.

Erik Doescher is a freelance illustrator based in Dallas, Texas. He attended the School of Visual Arts in New York City. Erik illustrated for a number of comic studios throughout the 1990s, and then moved to Texas to pursue videogame development and design. However, he has not given up on illustrating his favorite comic book characters.

Mike DeCarlo is a longtime contributor of comic art whose range extends from Batman and Iron Man to Bugs Bunny and Scooby-Doo. He resides in Connecticut with his wife and four children.

Lee Loughridge has been working in comics for more than fifteen years. He currently lives in sunny California in a tent on the beach.

GLOSSARY

atmosphere (AT-muhss-fihr)—the mixture of gases that surrounds a planet

counterclockwise (koun-tur-KLOK-wize)—in a direction opposite to the hands of a clock

database (DAH-tuh-bayss)—the information that is organized and stored in a computer

evidence (EV-uh-duhnss)—information or facts that help prove that something is true

horizon (huh-RYE-zuhn)—the line where the sky and the earth or sea seem to meet

identical (eye-DEN-ti-kuhl)—exactly the same

meteorological (mee-tee-ur-roh-LOJ-ih-kuhl)—having to do with the science of weather or climate

molecule (MOL-uh-kyool)—the smallest part of a substance that displays all the chemical properties of that substance

penitentiary (pen-uh-TEN-chur-ee)—a state or federal prison for people found guilty of crimes

phantom (FAN-tuhm)—a ghost

DISCUSSION QUESTIONS

1. Do you believe that the Weather Wizard started the tornado? Explain your answer.

2. The Flash trusted the Weather Wizard for a moment. Do you think this was a good decision? Why or why not?

3. If you had the power to control the weather, what type of weather would you choose? Do you like it sunny and warm, or cold and rainy? Why?

WRITING PROMPTS

1. Everyone has a favorite super hero! Write a list of your top three favorites. Why do you like them? Does the Flash make the list?

2. Do you think Flash will face the Weather Wizard again? Write a story about what would happen if they met a second time.

3. Imagine you could run as fast as the Flash. Where would you go? What places would you see? Write about having super-speed for a day!

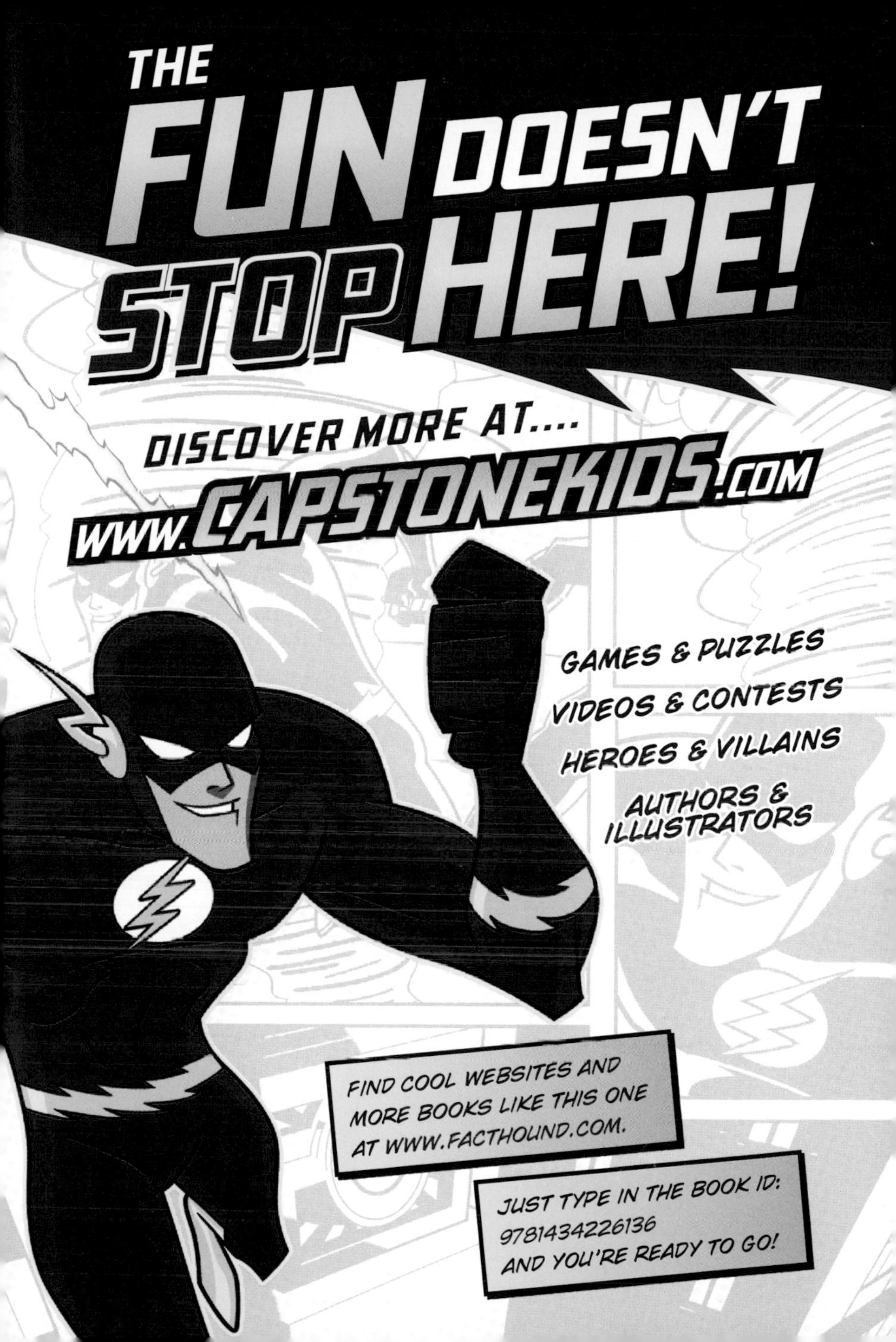
THE FUN DOESN'T STOP HERE!
DISCOVER MORE AT....
WWW.CAPSTONEKIDS.COM
GAMES & PUZZLES
VIDEOS & CONTESTS
HEROES & VILLAINS
AUTHORS & ILLUSTRATORS
FIND COOL WEBSITES AND MORE BOOKS LIKE THIS ONE AT WWW.FACTHOUND.COM.
JUST TYPE IN THE BOOK ID: 9781434226136 AND YOU'RE READY TO GO!

MORE NEW *The* FLASH™ ADVENTURES!

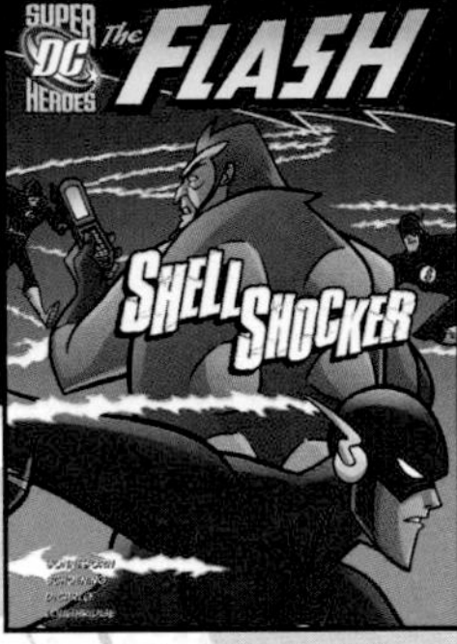
SUPER DC HEROES
The FLASH
SHELL SHOCKER

SHELL SHOCKER

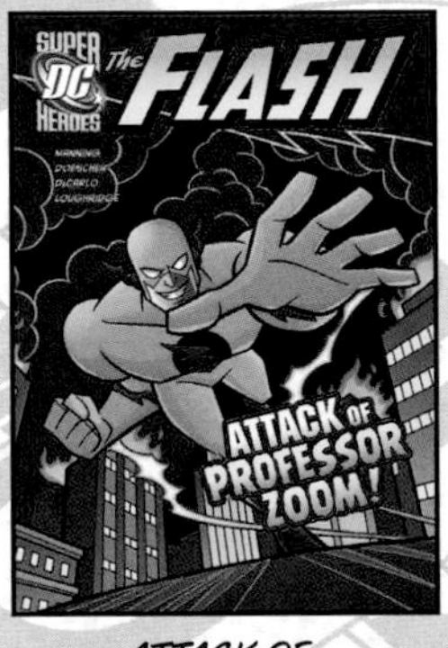
SUPER DC HEROES
The FLASH
MANNING
DOESCHER
DICARLO
LOUGHRIDGE
ATTACK OF PROFESSOR ZOOM!

ATTACK OF PROFESSOR ZOOM!

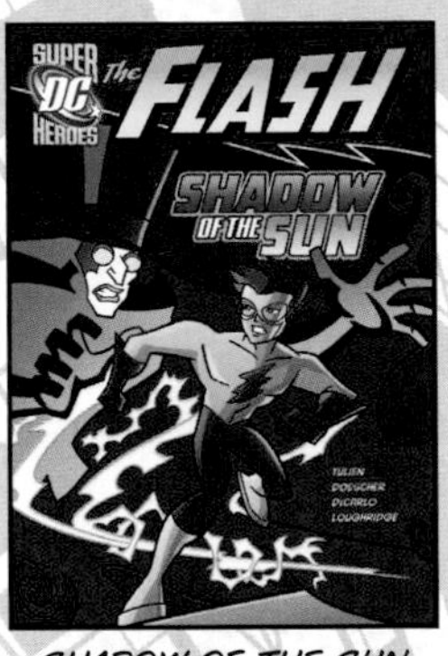
SUPER DC HEROES
The FLASH
SHADOW OF THE SUN
TULIEN
DOESCHER
DICARLO
LOUGHRIDGE

SHADOW OF THE SUN

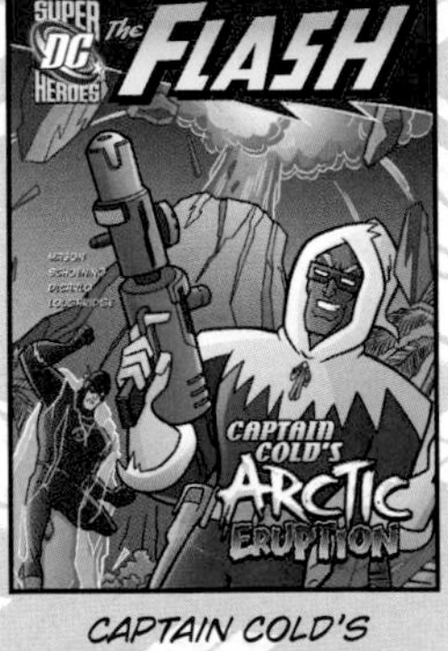
SUPER DC HEROES
The FLASH
CAPTAIN COLD'S ARCTIC ERUPTION

CAPTAIN COLD'S ARCTIC ERUPTION

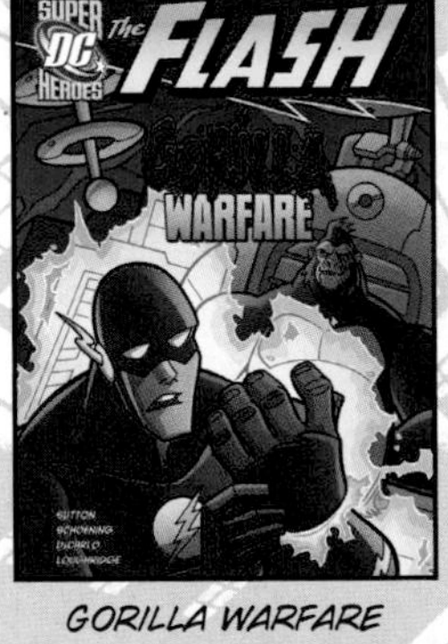
SUPER DC HEROES
The FLASH
WARFARE

GORILLA WARFARE

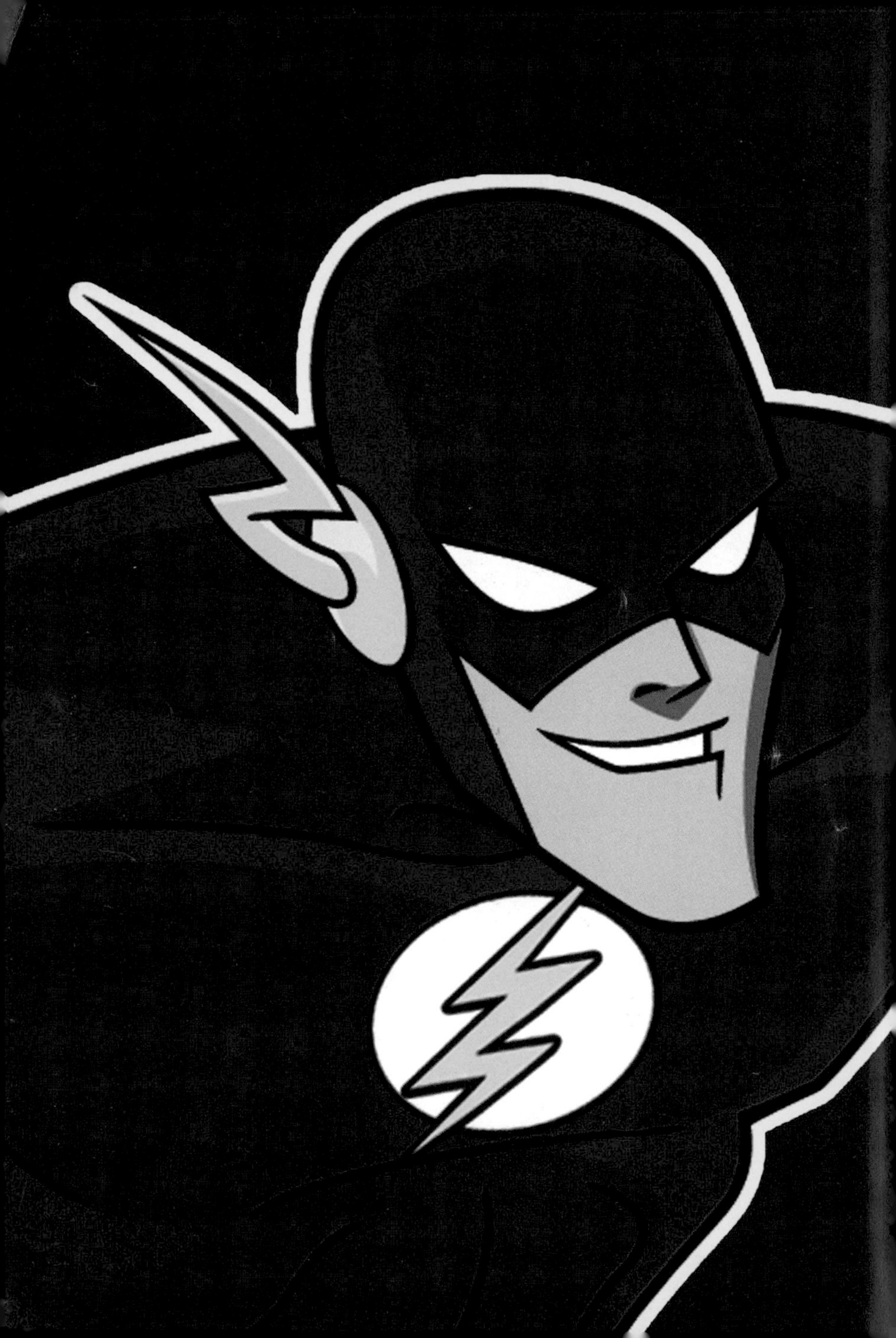